SEAN TAYLOR is an award-winning children's author and storyteller with wide experience of teaching creative writing. He has twice been shortlisted for the Roald Dahl Funny Prize, with *Purple Class and the Half-Eaten Sweater* and *Crocodiles Are the Best Animals of All*. His other books include *Purple Class and the Skelington*, *Purple Class and the Flying Spider*, *The Grizzly Bear with the Frizzly Hair*, *Who Ate Auntie Iris?*, *We Have Lift-Off*, *The Great Snake*, and the acclaimed debut teen novel *A Waste of Good Paper*. He lives in England and Brazil.

LAURENT CARDON has a background in film animation, but is now a full-time children's book illustrator. His picture books, including *Wolf Wanted*, are much admired internationally, and *That's What Makes a Hippopotamus Smile!* is his first picture book for Frances Lincoln Children's Books. He was born and brought up in France, and now lives in Brazil.

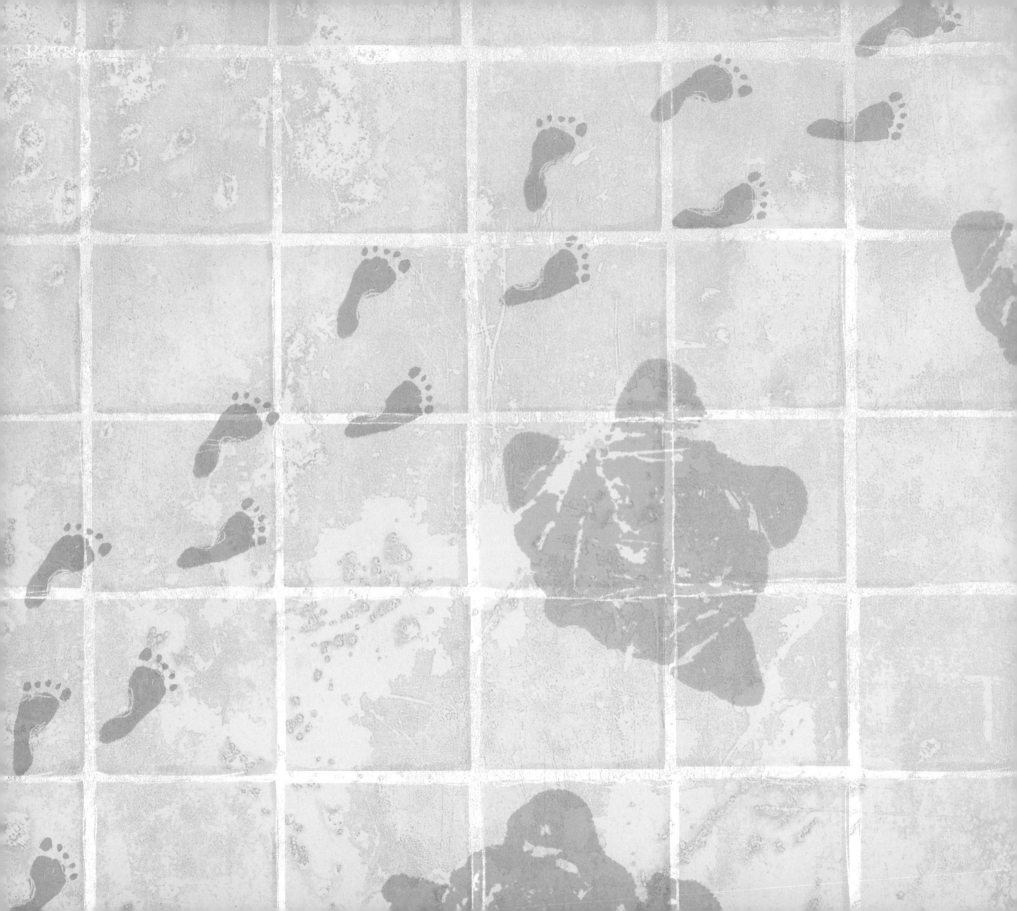

*For a teacher called Stuart, who started the day by getting Yellow Class
to sing the old campfire "Hippo Song"... and gave me the idea for this story – ST*

For all the imaginary animals we dreamed of, that liked having their backs scratched . . . – LC

Text copyright © Sean Taylor 2014
Illustrations copyright © Laurent Cardon 2014
The rights of Sean Taylor and Laurent Cardon to be identified respectively as the author and
illustrator of this work have been asserted by them in accordance with the Copyright,
Designs and Patents Act, 1988 (United Kingdom).

First published in Great Britain and in the USA in 2014 by
Frances Lincoln Children's Books, 74-77 White Lion Street, London N1 9PF
www.franceslincoln.com

First paperback published in Great Britain and in the USA in 2015

A catalogue record for this book is available from the British Library.

ISBN 978-1-84780-595-9

Illustrated with mixed ink techniques and digital art

Printed in China

1 3 5 7 9 8 6 4 2

That's What Makes a Hippopotamus Smile!

Written by
Sean Taylor

Illustrated by
Laurent Cardon

F

FRANCES LINCOLN
CHILDREN'S BOOKS

When a hippopotamus comes round to your house,
don't be worried, or *scared* by his size.
Just hug him and open the door very w i d e .

Because . . .

. . . that's what makes
a hippopotamus come inside!

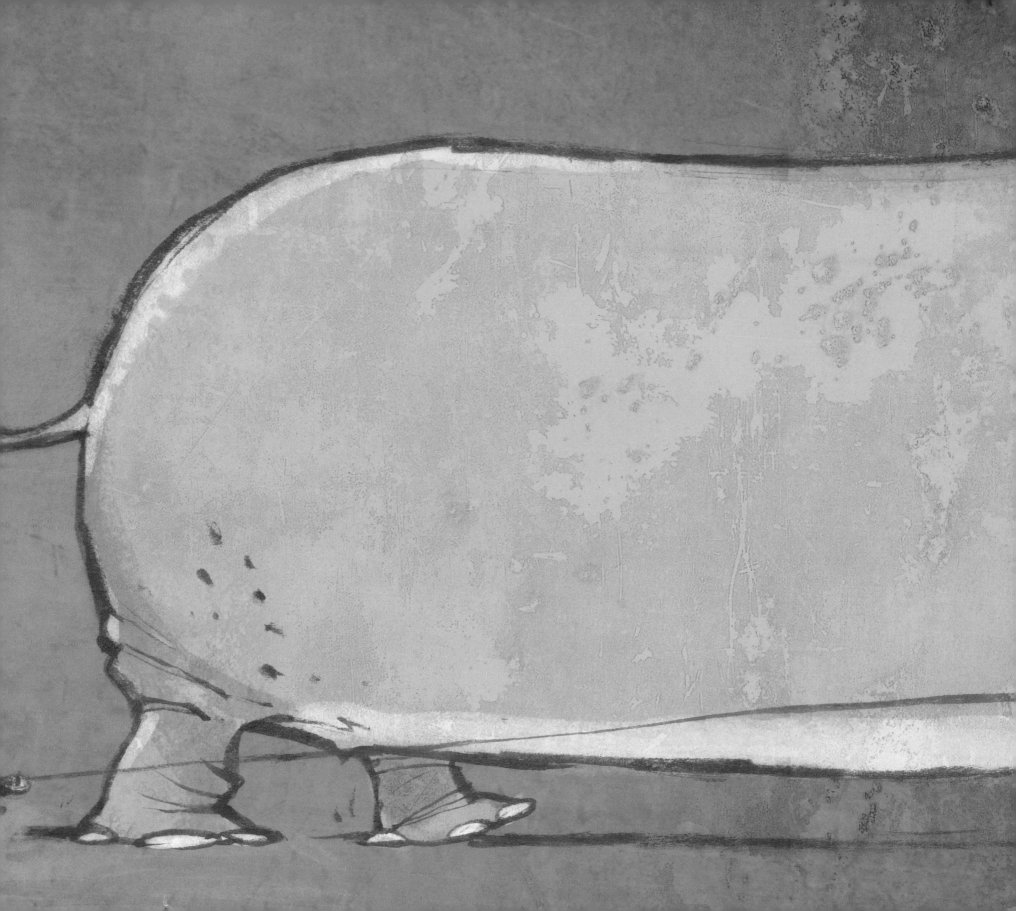

And when a hippopotamus wants to play a game,
don't make it quiet, clean or dry.
Choose something splishy, sploshy and splashy.

Because . . .

. . . that's what makes
a hippopotamus happy!

When you and the hippo need cleaning up,
remember that hippos love a good wash.
So share silly toys in a **big warm** bath.

Because . . .

. . . that's what makes
a hippopotamus laugh!

And after that, you'll both be hungry.
But don't eat popcorn, cookies or chips.
Have a great BIG crunchy salad-treat.

Because . . .

. . . that's what a hippopotamus loves to eat!

And when the hippo has to go home,
try not to be sad . . . even if you are.
Do a little dance.

Say goodbye in style.
Because . . .

... that's what makes
a hippopotamus smile!

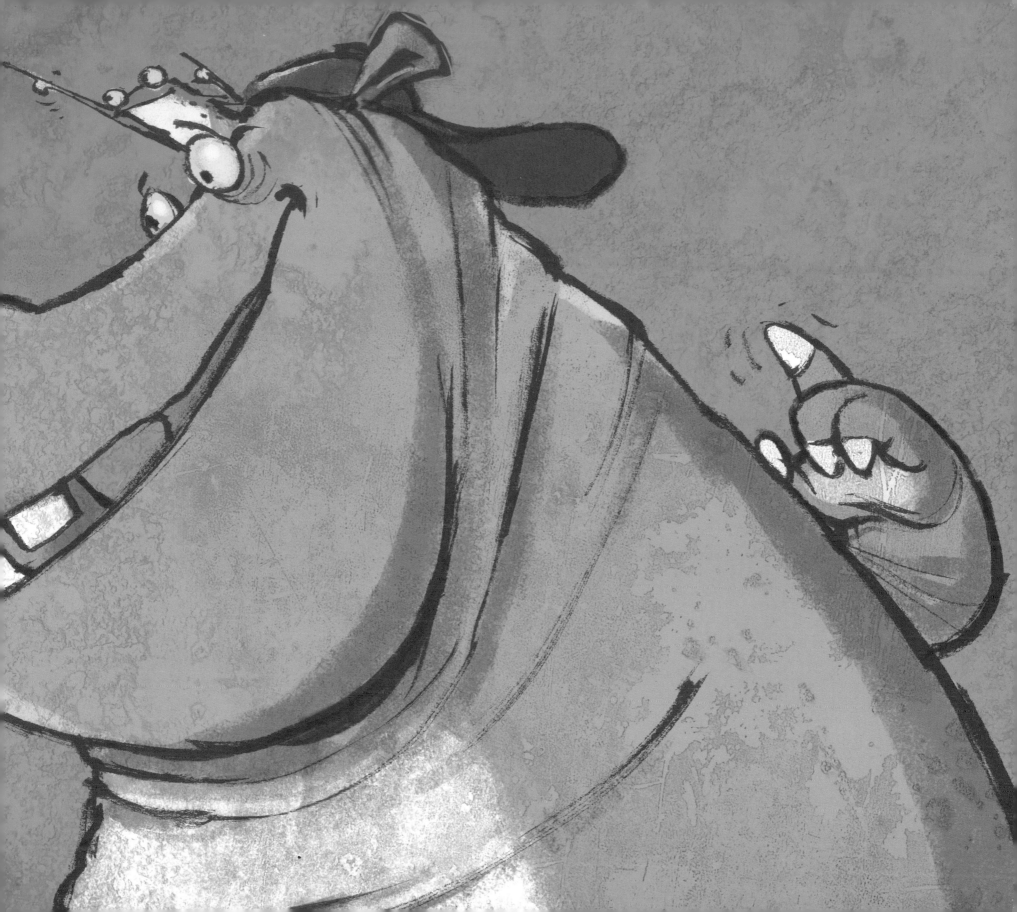

Then when the hippo thinks about you,
and of all the fun the two of you had,
he'll know that you're his
BEST NEW FRIEND.

And . . .

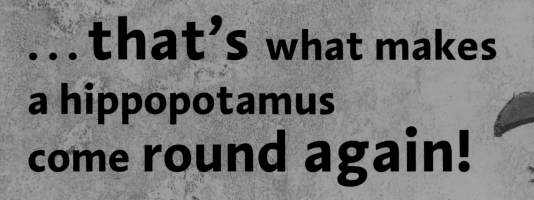

…**that's** what makes
a hippopotamus
come **round again!**

(Though maybe not just on his own . . .)

MORE GREAT PICTURE BOOKS BY SEAN TAYLOR PUBLISHED BY FRANCES LINCOLN CHILDREN'S BOOKS, ILLUSTRATED BY HANNAH SHAW

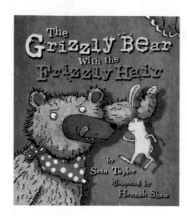

The Grizzly Bear with the Frizzly Hair
978-1-84780-144-9

"Fantastic comic appeal and full of drama"
– *Armadillo Magazine*

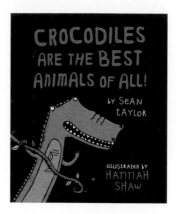

Crocodiles are the Best Animals of All
978-1-84780-132-6

Shortlisted for the Roald Dahl Funny Prize

"Picture book of the season" – *Bookseller*

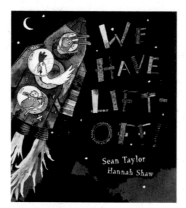

We Have Lift-Off!
978-1-84780-512-6

"Fun and lively, with a wonderful cast of animals"
– *Parents in Touch*

Who Ate Auntie Iris?
978-1-84780-314-6

Selected in Charlie Higson's Pick of Best Books
for Christmas

"A brilliant read-aloud adventure"- *Bookseller*

Frances Lincoln titles are available from all good bookshops.
You can also buy books and find out more about your favourite titles,
authors and illustrators on our website: www.franceslincoln.com